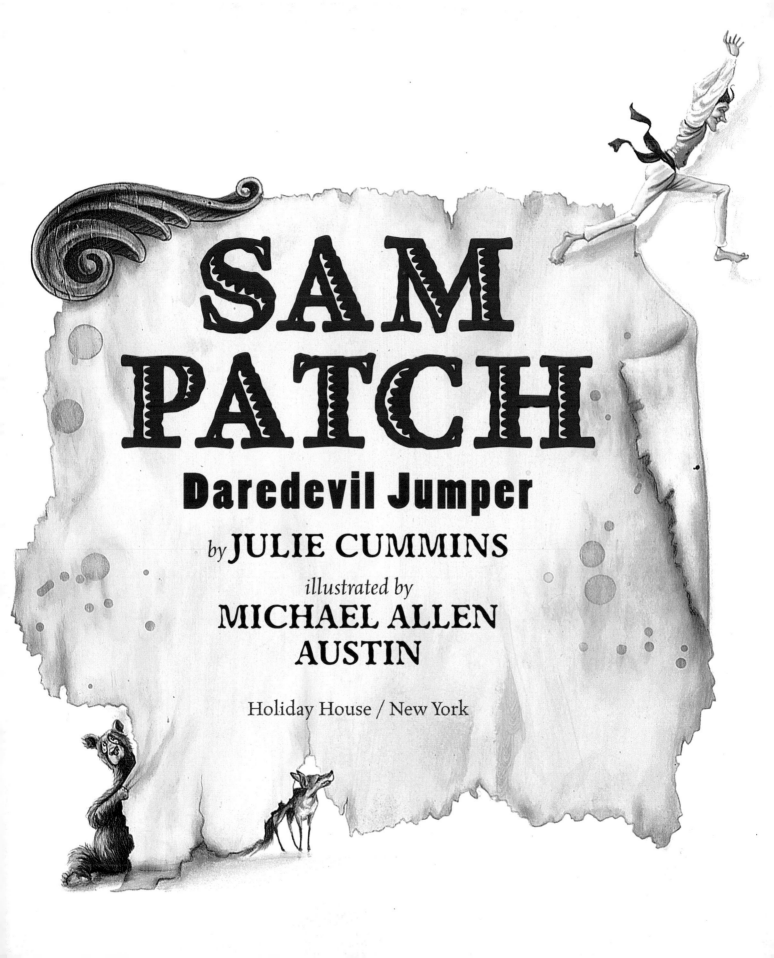

SAM PATCH

Daredevil Jumper

by JULIE CUMMINS

illustrated by
MICHAEL ALLEN
AUSTIN

Holiday House / New York

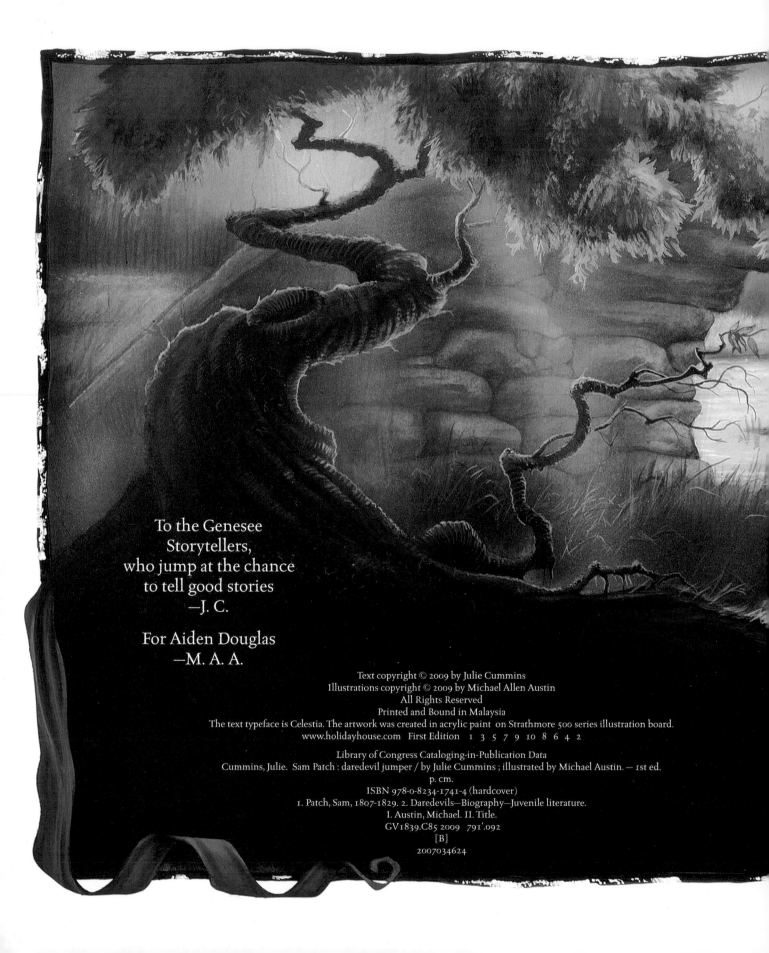

To the Genesee
Storytellers,
who jump at the chance
to tell good stories
—J. C.

For Aiden Douglas
—M. A. A.

Text copyright © 2009 by Julie Cummins
Illustrations copyright © 2009 by Michael Allen Austin
All Rights Reserved
Printed and Bound in Malaysia
The text typeface is Celestia. The artwork was created in acrylic paint on Strathmore 500 series illustration board.
www.holidayhouse.com First Edition 1 3 5 7 9 10 8 6 4 2
Library of Congress Cataloging-in-Publication Data
Cummins, Julie. Sam Patch : daredevil jumper / by Julie Cummins ; illustrated by Michael Austin. — 1st ed.
p. cm.
ISBN 978-0-8234-1741-4 (hardcover)
1. Patch, Sam, 1807-1829. 2. Daredevils—Biography—Juvenile literature.
I. Austin, Michael. II. Title.
GV1839.C85 2009 791'.092
[B]
2007034624

Sam Patch was a born jumper. Folks say that when he was born, he jumped right into his mother's arms. That was just the beginning.

Sam and his family lived in Pawtucket, Rhode Island, where a cotton mill flourished beside a waterfall. When Sam was knee-high to a grasshopper and could put one foot in front of the other, he would jump from any spot he could find—a fence, a ladder, a shed. If Sam could look up at it, he would jump from it. Mrs. Patch would smile and say, "That's my Sam; he's a natural jumper, jumpin' to beat all!"

When Sam was just a young boy, he went to work at a cotton mill. After their hard work was done for the day, the other young mill hands would swim in the river, diving from the bridge over it. Not Sam; he made running jumps from the mill roof into the Pawtucket River, almost 100 feet above the water. All those daring leaps as a young lad made Sam an expert swimmer as well as a jumper—something that he would put to dauntless use.

But the next thing Sam jumped into was a bad business deal. He had high hopes of earning a small fortune when he sank all his earnings into a cotton mill in Central Falls, Rhode Island. But his dreams were washed down the drain when his partner ran off with all the money.

Broke but brash, Sam headed to Paterson, New Jersey, to work as a spinner in a cotton mill. The mill was set on the picturesque Passaic Falls beside a chasm of considerable depth. That ravine would provide a natural setting for a natural jumper.

Sam marked the beginning of his career as a daredevil and showman jumper on September 30, 1827, in Paterson. On that day crowds gathered to watch the placing of the first bridge across the gorge. Sam gave them an unscheduled thrill. Hiding behind a tree to avoid the town constables, he suddenly darted out and jumped into the falls from the highest cliff—70 feet! The folks were amazed. They thought his leap was the best stunt they had ever seen, and Sam immediately became a known daredevil. Folks wasted no time in nicknaming him the Jersey Jumper. By popular demand he repeated his jump into the Passaic Falls in July 1828.

Sam's newly gained fame kept him from spinning much cotton, but he had more important—and higher—things to spin in his mind.

The next month he made a plunge from a platform atop the masthead of a sloop off Hoboken, New Jersey—a 90-foot jump.

Sam's motto was "Some things can be done as well as others." Word of his daring spread quickly. As his fame grew, he began to seek new heights to conquer. And the mighty Niagara Falls beckoned.

When Sam arrived at Niagara Falls, he didn't make quite the splash he had intended. He was the star attraction at an event on October 6, 1829, to celebrate the blasting off of a dangerous cliff that overhung the chasm—but he didn't show. Did he get cold feet? Not Sam! He just arrived a day late. So, instead of seeing the famous daredevil leap and live, the disappointed spectators had to settle for watching the other scheduled event—an old schooner that was sent crashing into the rapids.

Determined to prove his mettle, the very next day Sam made a 70-foot jump from the lower end of Goat Island into the falls, but the crowd was meager. Now, Sam prided himself on being a showman jumper. Not satisfied with this effort, he planned a greater spectacle. He plastered the region with signs advertising a leap into the falls on October 17—this time from a height of 120 feet.

On the day of the event, a crowd gathered to see if this daredevil could really prove his claim. Sam readied himself, took off his shoes and coat, and tied a black silk handkerchief around his neck. He boldly climbed the ladder to the scaffold. After ten minutes of testing the stand and displaying his bravado while the crowd cheered, he tied his handkerchief around his waist, kissed the American flag, waved to the crowd, and jumped—120 feet!

When Sam didn't immediately bob up in the churning water, a panic swept through the crowd. "He's dead! He's lost!" people cried. Other folks remained silent—until Sam's head and beaming face burst out of the water. Cheers and yells acclaimed Sam's stunt as his greatest triumph yet. Sam declared, "There's no mistake in Sam Patch!" Folks agreed; he became a national hero.

Sam believed he could now jump off any bridge or waterfall and even dreamed of jumping off London Bridge. But Rochester, New York, and the Genesee Falls were not far away, not far away at all.

While some would say that nothing could beat the mighty Niagara Falls, Sam was reaching for new heights and needed a fresh challenge. Rochester was a booming flour-mill town with the Genesee Falls positioned right on the newly built Erie Canal—providing exactly the kind of risk that Sam liked.

Sam arrived in Rochester in late October 1829 with his pet bear and pet fox. His fame and the handsome earnings from his jumps quickly drew the attention of a group of young sports promoters. Soon they had spread the word about the "jumpin' hero" who had come to town.

On October 29 the daily newspaper, prior to a local election, announced: "Another Leap. Sam Patch Against the World. He puts off the jump till after the election out of regard for all parties. Let every man do his duty at the polls and Sam will afterward do his at the Falls."

The date of the spectacle was set for November 6. Six to eight thousand people gathered at the Upper Falls of the Genesee to witness the 100-foot plunge. Sam, confident and jaunty, led his pet bear by a chain to the rock jutting over the falls. Without a second of hesitation, he sent the animal whirling into the water. The wide-eyed crowd whistled and shouted as the bear emerged and swam safely to the bank. Now they were primed for the main event.

Sam was poised. Wearing his black handkerchief sash and white pants, he bowed and leaped into the cataract. Folks held their breath, but within seconds Sam's head bobbed up several feet downstream. He waved off a small boat waiting to take him aboard, swam to shore, and waded up the bank—once again a hero.

With another triumph under his belt, Sam was feeling on top of the world. He planned a second and greater feat. By erecting a 25-foot platform on the rock above the falls, he planned to raise his jump to 125 feet! The event was advertised: "Higher Yet— Sam's Last Jump!"

To build up the excitement, Sam set the date for his jump for Friday, November 13! Superstitious? Not Sam; he was going to prove that nothing could jinx his jumping.

The day dawned cold and blustery. In spite of the raw weather, seven thousand people came from all over western New York—by stagecoach, canal boat, and horse and wagon, and on foot. They crowded around the riverbanks of the Genesee.

Promptly at two o'clock, Sam walked out onto the grassy rock. He wore a light jacket, a skull cap, and white pants that were part of a band uniform that he had borrowed from a friend. His signature black silk handkerchief was knotted around his waist.

There were some in the crowd who thought that Sam lacked his usual self-confidence when he climbed the scaffold. Some thought he swayed; some thought he shivered as if he was chilled.

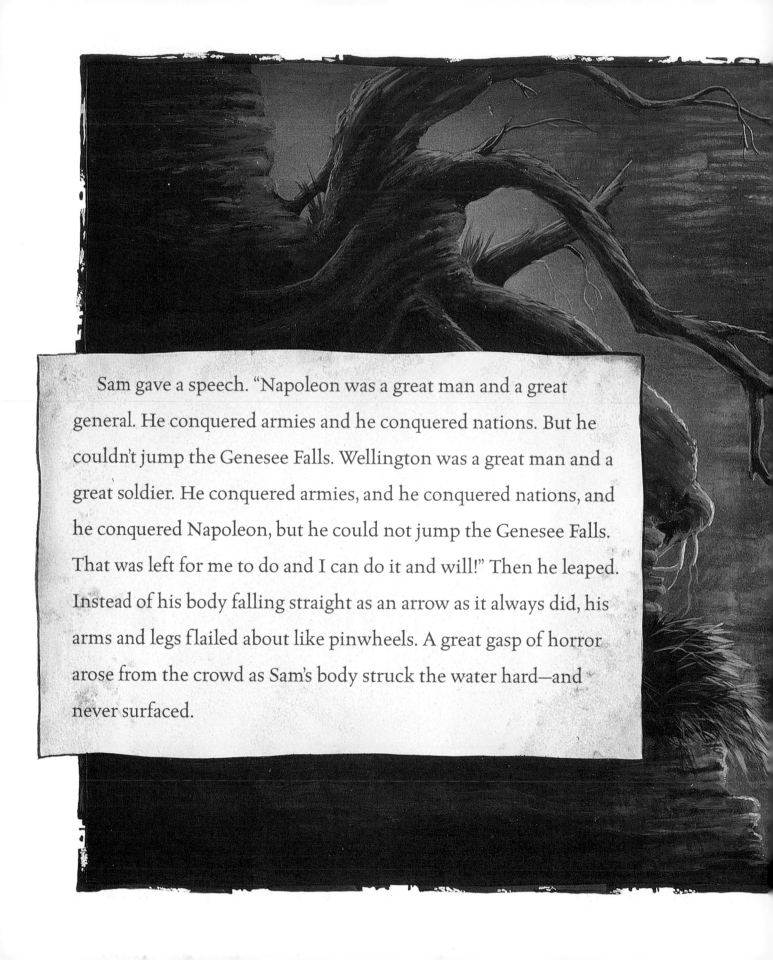

Sam gave a speech. "Napoleon was a great man and a great general. He conquered armies and he conquered nations. But he couldn't jump the Genesee Falls. Wellington was a great man and a great soldier. He conquered armies, and he conquered nations, and he conquered Napoleon, but he could not jump the Genesee Falls. That was left for me to do and I can do it and will!" Then he leaped. Instead of his body falling straight as an arrow as it always did, his arms and legs flailed about like pinwheels. A great gasp of horror arose from the crowd as Sam's body struck the water hard—and never surfaced.

The man who was a natural jumper, the man who was nicknamed the Jersey Jumper, the man who bested Niagara Falls, the man who jumped into waterfalls and into American legend—was never seen alive again.

The posters hailing his jump as his last had been prophetic. Sam Patch was born a jumper. Sam Patch died a jumper.

The river was searched in vain. Not until the following March was his body found. A farmer breaking ice in the river to water his horse found white pants and a black handkerchief that identified the frozen body. Sam was laid to rest in the old cemetery overlooking the falls where he had died. The marker on his grave said "Here lies Sam Patch. Such is fame."

Some folks say that at twilight on November 13, if you look out over the Genesee Falls, you can see a figure with a black handkerchief around the waist, poised on a rock, ready to jump.

HISTORICAL NOTE

Sam Patch was a real person who did indeed make all those jumps. Researching facts about people who lived a long time ago sometimes requires its own small leap of faith, as documents don't always agree. For example, some sources list the date of Sam's first jump into Niagara Falls as October of 1828, while others give the year as 1829. So the author must weigh the information and use the sources she feels are most reliable.

Born in 1807, Sam Patch lived in a world where television didn't exist and daredevils were a major form of entertainment. He was twenty-two years old when he died on that fateful November 13, 1829; and he is buried in the Charlotte Cemetery in Rochester, New York. Sam was a folk hero who became a folk legend, who jumped right into the hearts of Americans—those who saw him, those who heard tales of his magnificent jumping, and those who read about him.

SOURCE NOTES

Each source note includes the first word or words and the last word or words of a quotation and its source. References are to articles cited in the Selected Bibliography.

"Some things . . . others." *Rochester Democrat and Chronicle,* November 13, 1979.

"He's dead . . . lost!" *Rochester Democrat and Chronicle,* October 14, 1945.

"There's . . . Sam Patch!" *Rochester Times-Union,* November 14, 1929.

"Napoleon . . . and will!" *Rochester Democrat and Chronicle,* November 13, 1979.

SELECTED BIBLIOGRAPHY

Condon, George E. *Stars in the Water: The Story of the Erie Canal.* Garden City, NY: Doubleday & Co., 1974.

Dorson, Richard M. *America in Legend: Folklore from the Colonial Period to the Present.* New York: Pantheon Books, 1973.

Klees, Emerson. *Legends and Stories of the Finger Lakes Region: The Heart of New York State.* Rochester, NY: Friends of the Finger Lakes Publishing, 1995.

The Life Treasury of American Folklore. New York: Time, Inc., 1961.

Merrill, Arch. "Daredevil's Antics Once Boomed City," *Rochester Democrat and Chronicle* (NY), October 14, 1945.

——. *Down the Lore Lanes: Oddities in Upstate History.* New York: American Book-Stratford Press, 1961.

Myers, Jim. "Sam Patch: 150 Years Ago Sam Leaped off Genesee Falls for Last Time," *Rochester Democrat and Chronicle* (NY), November 13, 1979.

Rogers, Glenn A. *Forgotten Stories of the Finger Lakes: Dramatic Tales of Fact and Legend.* Geneva, NY: A. Glenn Rogers, 1954.

Thomason, Caroline W. "Sam Patch Made Noted Leap over Falls Here Just One Century Ago," *Rochester Times-Union* (NY), November 14, 1929.